THE RUNAWAY NOTE

Second Edition

THE RUNAWAY NOTE

copyright © 2012 Tyrone Jaeger

second edition © 2018

ISBN-13: 978-0-9967788-2-4

ISBN-10: 0-9967788-2-9

Shakespeare & Company, Toad Suck

Arkansas USA

Shakespeare & Co. Toad Suck books
are designed and published
by Mark Spitzer
sptzr.net

ACKNOWLEDGMENTS

Thanks to the editors of the following journals, who published pieces from this collection, sometimes in different forms and with different titles: *580 Split, The Cupboard, Exquisite Corpse Annual, Indiana Review, Nimrod International Journal, ONTHEBUS, PRISM INTERNATIONAL, Southeast Review,* and *West Branch Wired.*

Thanks to my lovely wife Julee for the author photo, the coyote stitching, her patience, and the inspiration she offers me.

TABLE OF CONTENTS

For us

THE RUNAWAY NOTE

THE INQUISITION

A flying saucer burns two eye-shaped holes in the hayfield. The eyes follow us wherever we go. Mother keeps a lucky penny in her shoe and tallies crows with the fervor of an auctioneer. She swallows the milk of superstition. She illustrates fortune and omen and draws the curtains in nightshade.

I am writing a runaway note on my red typewriter. A stranger knocks and introduces himself as Colonel Rip Van Scratch. He stinks of whiskey and jet fuel. He's got eyes like holes burned by a flying saucer. The Colonel says, Rumors are the boy's marked as mine. Mother says, Tyro's a good boy and I should know. She points to the umbilical cord that connects us.

Mother searches my head for horns or 666. She says, Phrenologically speaking, he reads like a bald tire, slick and temperamental. She fixes my hair with hairspray. Colonel Scratch says, That's flammable, you know. Mother says, That's not flammable, that's a cowlick.

1

THE RUNAWAY NOTE

The Colonel throws me on the kitchen table, spreading me out like a treasure map. His hands feel like every truth I never wanted to hear. He scratches at the course of my heart—straights and narrows, switchbacks, and the inevitable dead end.

The Colonel says, The boy's destiny is written in a third nipple, and a stray patch of hair flanking his lower ribcage, and the howler is this coyote-shaped birthmark. Mother says, That's no sign of the beast, that's a beauty mark.

The Colonel says, He's writing a runaway note. Mother says, That's no runaway note, that's his memoirs. Tyro's sensitive like that. His grandmother could talk a squirrel down from a tree, and he talks himself up into a state of susceptibility. When he's on a typing roll, he gets so sensitive, he catches cold by dreaming it.

Outside, Colonel Scratch's red van bathes in moonlight. *Sin Bin* painted on the side. I say, I've no plans to travel with the likes of you. Scratch tips his hat to Mother. He says, Beware of the signs. *Sass, truancy, and silence.*

THE RUNAWAY NOTE

He rides his motorcycle out the back of the Sin Bin. I continue my runaway note, a litany of sufferings, shortcomings, and unfulfilled aspirations. Mother mops up Scratch's boot marks. She says, Why he's taller than I ever imagined. I say, To hell with his stature. He's got plans to enlist me as a backscratcher, a backslapper, a bootlicker. Mother ignores me and kneads dough, her cheeks rosy.

I wake to snow. I break a dream over my knee. Outside, the Sin Bin looks like the flames of destiny. There are no tracks in the snow but the driver's seat feels warm. I pull the shifter into neutral. Headlights off, I coast into the night.

A pack of coyotes follow at every turn. I stop at the dam site, and the coyotes yowl. I step out and they surround me. I hand the leader my runaway note. It says: *I'm going to run away tomorrow morning when you are sleeping. Be sure to say goodbye forever.* The coyotes lift their chins and offer their apologies to the moon.

RUMORS OF GREATNESS

In the Kaats Kills, they fear my name. I am Tyro of the red typewriter. I am the boy with no heart. They call me ruthless and cruel. They say I drive nails into my feet and tap dance to the songs of crying babies. I've been known to yodel in the shower and cheat at solitaire. I've been known to cavort with Morisa.

They say Morisa worships the moon. They say she makes boys loony with the geometry of her open legs. It's no lie. She'll lead them to the dam site, and I stand behind a tree and aim my slingshot. We leave their naked bodies on the church steps.

They say her mother's a drunk and a cat lady who married the funeral director for make-up tips. The bandies cluck that we got no sense of propriety and no shame. To think what they'd say if they saw us rolling about in the cemetery! The ghosts we conjure. The coyotes and vultures we attract.

When I get Morisa laughing, she gets humid with humor. The scent gets me yawping and typing and standing on one foot. Oh, she's got it all! Back straight, chest out, eyes to the ground in search of dollar bills!

And how to describe her face? It is an invitation to sin. Eyes selfish like a cat's. Breath that stirs my blood like wind rouses the clouds. Morisa says, Don't worry, darling. You stick with me and you'll see the worst of it. Indeed, a healthy oyster never produces a pearl.

It's all true, what the bandies say. We lie, cheat, and steal. We cut the heads off chickens to see where they keep the eggs. Imagine a pearl you can suck the yoke out of. Imagine how yellow the taste of her mouth. The scratch of a just-formed claw.

SCISSORS, PASTE, AND THE DEAD

Great Granny took scissors to two photographs as if to make paper dolls: the first her dead parents, and the second her boy, buried at age five. She pasted the clipped photos onto a photograph of her man, her girl, and herself. Three dead stand in the foreground, aligned with the living—mothers, fathers and children each in a row, one dead to one alive. The girl holds a baby doll that looks to the sky and appears to be screaming.

After the boy died, they moved from Dog Hill to Huntersfield. Sometimes the dead do not leave a place, and the living must relocate. When the living relocate the dead, it's called reinterment. When the dead relocate the living, it's called sadness. In the Kaats Kills it was *two rocks to one dirt,* so farmers built stonewalls, monuments to the rigid geometry of division: meadow to woods, freed to penned, living to dead.

In the photograph, the boy wears a sailor's suit and a vaporous smile that says, I will die soon, and then I will walk among you. His death haunted Great Granny, drove her to drink, and to suspect her girl of being alive. She was a living *daughter*, not a dead son. She walked outside the photograph. She was not glued. For this, she was not forgiven. She was charged and duly punished. Forgiveness privileges the dead.

Life tasted of two rocks to one dirt, a bitter ratio tempered by the soft teats of cows, warm milk, and steaming shit. Days tasted of glue made from flour and cement used to bury the living with the dead. Boys wear sailor suits, and even in black and white, we recognize royal blue and yellow hair. We recognize the dead among the living. Here, *this* is ghost, and *this* is living, little girl.

When the dead visit the living, we call it a haunting. When the dead visit the living, they are called ghosts, not visitors. Ghosts haunt. When the living impose life on the dead (that is, when the living invite the dead to live), what is this called? A séance is the wrong answer. The dead do not RSVP. They lack pens, they lack stamps, they lack vocal cords. Great Granny outlived her boy and her girl. She birthed two children and hundreds of calves, but only one did she pray to be reborn.

When I die, I will haunt those I love. I will haunt Morisa, the woman I will someday marry. I will whisper that I love her. I will whisper, Don't be afraid. I will whisper, Find the photograph of me, the one where I'm not smiling, and paste it onto a picture of you, next to you.

I will tell her that I miss her, that ghosts fill the afterlife, that when she dies, I will see her. Love in the afterlife is like fog rising. All these things, I will tell her.

THE RUNAWAY NOTE

NO HEART, TWO HEARTS, THREE

If you ever saw Morisa do the Watusi, you too would bend down on all fours and sniff out trespass and sin. For her, I steal deer antlers from living room walls. For her, I hoard my fingernail clippings. I rob frogs of their eyes and bats of their wings. On Valentine's I give her Great Granny's picture with the dead glued in with the living.

Morisa believes in equal protection under the law and therefore the liberation of the dead. She says that even a dead boy must have a heart. She pokes me in the chest. Only a fool would resist her schemes. She's promised me the worst of it. At the dam, Morisa casts a spell with muddy water and pulp scraped from our hearts. She commands my dead uncle to step from the photograph. Fog rises from the picture.

Standing before us, the dead boy stretches his arms and yawns. A butterfly flits from his mouth. He follows Morisa around as if he's a lost puppy. She names him Sailor Boy. We baptize him at the dam, in the reservoir where a town once was. I point to the foundation of a house. Morisa says, That's where we'll live! Sailor Boy asks if we're running away. He asks if we've kidnapped him. I say, You've been spirited away, but we ask no ransom. We swim out to the underwater house and float all night. There's no roof and the stars look lonely.

I ask Sailor Boy to tell us his history, and Morisa laughs and laughs, for she knows that history is like a foggy dream that you try to write down in the morning but are unable to find a pencil and while searching in the couch cushions you come across a love letter addressed to someone else and smelling of a perfect stranger who you will perhaps fall in love with.

THE RUNAWAY NOTE

SAILOR BOY SPEAKS

Sailor Boy says, When I slipped from the womb, the good doctor, Colonel Rip Van Scratch, slapped my ass, and I commenced to singing and counting. This led to the expectation that I might someday rival Blind Tom, the knife thrower. I spent my days catching caterpillars, all drunk on milkweed perfume. Nights, I captured fireflies by the thousands.

One night, I awoke with terrible pain, my skull an egg about to crack. Momma called the Colonel, who said, God sees fit to divide us into healthy and diseased, living and dead. To prove his point, the Colonel pulled out his doctor's log and began to read: *Mumps are showing themselves thick and fast in Big Hollow. Charles White has a child sick with brain fever. Last week Dr. Whitebeck of Hudson tapped a man named Haney in the town of Livingston, who was suffering from Dropsy and drew from him six gallons of clear water. The patient is doing well. When Levi Bailey served his guests cake, how was he to know that the cream of tartar package contained arsenic and the arsenic contained cream of tartar? It seems the two papers holding the two powders were inside a third, marked cream of tartar. As Levi now contests, To label is to live.*

How Momma screamed when the first butterflies crawled from my mouth and nose. I said, Momma, I didn't know ceasing was such agony. Ole Sawbones wrote *Death by Metamorphosis* in his log.

Momma hit the sauce, mixed it up with paint thinner and engine oil. She mowed down the milkweed, set the barn on fire, and pulled the plug on the beaver dam. Now a ghost, I called out, Momma, Stop the fuss! The body's nothing but a vessel for death! She was too looped on paint thinner to hear, too mean to bother haunting.

THE RUNAWAY NOTE

I was dead and dreaming makes me alive. I found a mirror that does not reflect your face but shows a map of your transmigrations. I walk with trespass and sin, following the backward course of history. I know an underwater town where you can get drunk with ghosts and ride the back of a giant walleye. I know a dead girl who does the Watusi. For five dollars, she will distinguish between resurrection and reincarnation. For three dollars more, she will hold your hand while you cry from missing your former selves.

THE RUNAWAY NOTE

A FAMILY ROMANCE

I wake like most mornings to the crash of that demented motorcyclist killing my dog. Now Sailor Boy and me watch cartoons. Underdog shines shoes then flies over tall buildings. Daddy says it's how piss-ants spend the morning. He sweeps up the glass. Next to the stonewall, he digs a hole. Me and Sailor Boy in our underwear get dew-soaked. Daddy drops the dog in the hole. He scatters the glass. I say, It looks like diamonds. Daddy says, It looks like another dead dog. He says, It looks like a hole that needs filling.

Mother gives a yank to my umbilical. She pulls me back inside. Sailor Boy's got a hole in his belly. I got a rope like a length of sausage. Mother makes pickled beets. She makes me turn off the TV. Sailor Boy finds a bobby pin, and I stick it in the socket. The jolt sets me on my ass. I damn God, like when Daddy slips a wrench. Mother sees the bobby pin and slaps my head. Her fingers are stained purple. I say, You made me bleed. She says, I'll give you something to bleed about.

THE RUNAWAY NOTE

When Mother cuts my hair, she snips my ear. I don't cry until she shows me the blood. I damn her, like she damns Daddy when he's hiding in the barn. She snips the cord at my belly. Blood drips on the kitchen floor. She reaches up under her skirt and snips once more. I run out the kitchen. She whips my cord and catches my foot. I spill like milk. She says, Don't forget your apron strings! I run to Daddy and he wipes the blood with an oil rag. I whip Sailor Boy with my cord. I kill a frog with my whip. I knock a bird from the sky.

In the barn, Daddy says I can use the grinder on rusty nails. It shoots sparks like a rocket. Sailor Boy picks butterflies from the barn windows. Daddy fixes the electric fence from where the horse pushed through. Sailor Boy plays with a dead monarch. Daddy calls us outside. He grabs me with one hand and the fence with the other. It feels like a whip inside me. Daddy says, It ain't no worse than a slap. Sailor Boy rolls on the ground laughing. I beat him with my cord. He spits in the dirt. He stands on the salt lick, blows on his fingers, and the dead monarch flies.

Sailor Boy and I play murderers' row inside the falling-down chicken coop. We have Morisa as the captive. She steps on a nail and gets the tetanus. Now, Sailor Boy carries the gas and I carry the hose. Daddy throws the match. The chicken coop burns the color of a banty. Mother's face turns red. She hides her hands. She pretends not to cry. Sailor Boy and I throw rocks into the fire. With a locked jaw and a rusty tongue, Morisa cries for me to push her on the swing.

Sailor Boy and I find a pillowcase full of kittens. We already have a barn full. Daddy fetches the twenty-two. Sailor Boy carries the pick and I carry the shovel. The field is a hungry mouth that's eaten dogs, cats, and horses. You got to shovel the mouth open. Days later, Sailor Boy and I dig up the litter. The kittens are covered in maggots and mucous. My legs welt from Daddy's belt. Sailor Boy feels no pain.

The hayfield has two eye-shaped shapes where grass won't grow. Spaceships came for grandmother. She let deer, owls, and raccoons live in the house. Once, an owl ate Mother's sock. Grandma's crow rode on the hood of Grandpa's car. Grandma had sickness upon sickness upon another sickness. Grandpa kept the crow drunk all day. They gave Grandma electricity for her sadness. Sailor Boy is her dead brother. He says, The angels live in flying saucers.

We had a dog that bit Sister's face. Later, that dog fought a porcupine. Daddy pulled the quills out with needle-nose pliers. The dog cried but didn't bite. He died of demonic mange. We give Daddy a pound puppy for his birthday. The first night, the puppy cries because it's tied up outside. Daddy beats him quiet. We are silent for days. Daddy and the dog train one another. The dog drags a woodchuck on the lawn. The dog chews a deer leg. Sailor Boy gets Sister to fetch it. Daddy throws the shovel for me to bury it. Sailor Boy digs it up and makes a baton to conduct our jug band. He sings, Life! Life! Life is holes that need making and holes that need filling!

Daddy drives us to the dam site. We steal a pick-up bed full of gravel. Grandpa works the reservoir gates. He sends the water down to New

York City. Daddy, Sailor Boy, and I cast some rods.
Daddy catches a bass. Sailor Boy catches a trout. I
catch a hook in my eyebrow and start to cry. Daddy
says, It ain't even bleeding. Daddy tosses beer cans in
the water. He promises us ice cream. Sailor Boy and
I promise not to tell Mother. We piss in the water.
The guinea-wops in the city will drink it.

Daddy takes us to see a dead dog in a tree. You
done this, he says. I punch Sailor Boy's arm. I don't
deny a thing. The bark is black with the dog's blood.
Sailor Boy ties a ribbon around the dog's neck. I slip
a turkey feather through the ribbon. Daddy sets the
dog on fire. Our sins are in the smoke. The smoke
rises to the sky. Jesus inhales it. He will exhale it
clean. We forget about the ice cream. Mother makes
the best strawberry shortcake. We eat until we're
red as berries. It starts to rain. Daddy, Sailor Boy, and
I take showers beneath the barn eves. It's a thunder
and lightning storm, but Daddy says that we've been
forgiven.

I've got a cousin who's an old man now. He's spent his life not saying anything to anybody, not even his mother. But he knows how to birth a calf, how to murder a crow, and how to wake a vulture. At night, my cousin runs through the woods. He doesn't even use a flashlight. He sees everything you imagine. Everything you dream. People think it a shame that he don't talk to his own mother. But Daddy, Sailor Boy, and I know better. When you subdue a man, his heart becomes hoary.

THE RUNAWAY NOTE

DEAR KAATS KILLS

They say that for six days God labored at creating the world. On the seventh day, he threw stones at the Kaats Kills. I hope it hurt like hell. I hope it's an itch you can't scratch. I won't stand for two rocks to one dirt. I'm going to where the sun shines and the buffalo roam. I'm driving a Barracuda, fish-tailing on the horseshoe bend. You won't make a Kaats Killer of me.

Yours Always,

Tyro

THE RUNAWAY NOTE

$25K IN UNMARKED BILLS

I've got big Wild West plans, but I've been stuck in my childhood trance for years. Daddy watches TV, turns up the volume, and changes the channel, a show about plastic surgery, home improvements for the flesh, dream it up and they will carve it. I slip a bandana over my face and light a banana of a cigar. I steal a jar of Mother's pickles and go out driving. Like the cowboys of old, I'll sleep under the stars, brew coffee in a saucepan, and enter towns just to rob them.

At the Stop-N-Go a bona-fide masked bandit points a gun at my head. I hand over my greenbacks and say, Hey mister, you got room in the back of that there car? Tied up fetal in the trunk, I spy the sunset through a rust hole. I try to shout, Yipee! but I cough on my gag. When we get to where the getting's good, we'll have a big laugh about this whole episode. I can't wait to see the bandit's face when I show him the runaway note I've carried all these years.

THE RUNAWAY NOTE

My stomach lurches when I hear Morisa's laughter up front. Sailor sings shanties. The Colonel spits. I hear coyotes snapping their teeth. I hear a nightmare unfolding like a letter dropped in the mailbox that you never should have written. I see the moon in the rust hole, the lunar landscape a mirror of my indignity.

THE RUNAWAY NOTE

A SWIM WITH THE COLONEL

The Colonel and I stand where flying saucers burned two eye-shaped holes in the hayfield. We each walk inside a different hole. We orbit in opposite directions, and though we don't say it, this makes us lonely.

The Colonel says, The universe is infinite and expanding, or perhaps contracting. He says, Time is only relevant for so long. He says, In the beginning was the Word. I say, What word was that?

The Colonel says, In the beginning the earth was without form, and void, and darkness was upon the face of the deep. I say, Must have been hard to read the Word in the darkness.

The Colonel says, Boy, spend less time chawing sass, and more time mulling your future. I point to the vultures flying overhead. The Colonel says, They follow wherever I go.

We drive the van to the dam site. We swim out to the underwater town. Looking down is like a God-eye view. We float on our backs. The vultures ride the thermals in lazy circles.

The Colonel says, You had no right to raise the boy. I say, He knows the way back, and besides, he likes his resurrection. The Colonel says, There's a difference between the resurrected and the undead. He says, That girl you run with has a thing for cemeteries and spells. I say, Don't we all trespass this life?

We float on our backs and the vultures circle and circle until I am hypnotized. The Colonel grabs my hand and pulls me under. We are forever in our sinking. I think, This is what it's like before waking. This is what it's like to be truly scared or in love.

We stand at the door of an underwater house. Fish the size of men swim through the windows. Eels rise like smoke from the chimney.

THE RUNAWAY NOTE

From behind me, the Colonel presses a hand over my eyes and another over my mouth. He blows bubbles into my ear, words that pop: Do. Not. Arouse. The. Sleeping. The Colonel disappears.

I try to swim away, but my legs won't kick. My arms won't paddle. I glide and glide. I see my shadow on the reservoir floor. It's shaped like a vulture with wings outspread. I glide in a circle. My shadow orbits below me.

Around the underwater house swim a school of my selves. They swim in a circle. Their shadows go round and round, like a kettle of vultures. Selves and shadows, riding the thermals. We continue like this. We carry on. We wake.

THE RUNAWAY NOTE

THE HORN THAT SPEARED ME

I wake up like most mornings aching from the horn that speared me. Morisa says that it's got nothing to do with flying saucers, but then why do I taste space in my cereal? Why do my clothes reek of jet fuel?

For Halloween Morisa's father paints us up like the dead who are painted to look like they are living. We knock on the back of the Colonel's van. He opens the door in a union suit. He appears out of breath. His fingers are covered in red. We hold out our baskets. Trick or treat, we say. He drags us inside and demands an explanation. I was deep in thought, he says. He shows us piles of letters, notes from the dead.

The Colonel sticks red pens in our hands. He says, Get busy. He says, I need a nap. He sleeps behind the wheel. Morisa and I draw houses and stick figures, flowers and rainbows. We draw each other behind desks, in cubicles, in church pews, in caskets. We draw each other in the back seat. We draw each other naked.

We draw on each other naked: flying saucer, clock, butterfly, vulture. And like that, the spirit overcomes us. Our hands move. We write dictation for the dead.

The sensation is like a velvet glove massaging your foot, like strawberry juice dripping off your tongue, like a tiny bell in the forest, like burnt ram upon the altar, like words upon the page. We write until they have finished speaking.

THE RUNAWAY NOTE

LETTER TO YOU, DURING THIS OUR NEW REINCARNATION

Morisa, I remember you best as a soldier on the run, back when we were still both men, both desperate. You, now a woman, and I, still a man. You were a deserted Redcoat, two trout on a string, a man free of war. I snuck behind you, stealth my only strength, and gagged you, brought you home to my shack. I had no idea what to do with you, torture or free you, hand you over to the Colonel.

In the night, you cut through the ropes and attacked me in my sleep. You cupped my mouth, hand stinking of trout and an onion I imagined you had eaten like an apple. You cussed into my ear—your breath creek mint—whispered something about salvation, and I wondered then how one might save time.

You slit my throat with my own knife, my blood our baptism into a religion I had only seconds to appreciate. You freed my dogs and loosed my horses. Coyotes howled beneath the window. The moon-shadow of a vulture traveled across the wall.

You soon returned, my eyes still open, my heart still aware. Bubbles formed on my lips in red blooms you could not resist. Bending down on one knee, you lifted my head. I shook, an angel without wings, and you held me tighter than my wife ever had. You left a funeral pyre of my home.

Now, you are beneath me, your eyes blaze fear as I tell this story of our past, of the pilgrimage we both made from so long ago. Do you think I seek revenge, an eye for an eye, a throat for a throat? That life, so far away, cannot be rectified. The past is nothing but a recipe for danger. I've tied you up only so that you may kiss my scars, heal me like you once did, but promise me that this time you'll not escape, that you'll not abandon me, and set my house afire.

THE RUNAWAY NOTE

A DANCE WITH THE COLONEL

I am writing my runaway note when outside the Sin Bin roars like a barn fire. A shoe breaks through the window. There is a note that reads *REEL?*

On my bicycle, I chase the Colonel down. Coyotes surround him, and he flirts shamelessly with me and the dogs. He says, Here for your dance lesson? He grabs me. The coyotes howl and snap their teeth like castanets. Sailor Boy appears and spots us with his jar of fireflies.

Too much spinning gets me featherbrained. I say, The darn fool's about to dip me! Sailor Boy laughs and says, Me next! Me next!

The Colonel throws me back, and I face the sky: Jupiter, Venus, and Hale-Bopp. Space dust catches fire, and I make a wish.

THE RUNAWAY NOTE

The Colonel drops me and says, You shouldn't have done that. I was about to teach you the mirror reel, and you wish to be somewhere else. The Colonel is long in the tooth and smells of carrion. I've got no time for dancing, I say.

He says, I gave you typing lessons and this is how you repay me? You'll get yours when I'm dead, I say. Still, he says, I thought us friends could have some fun. Let me take your van for a spin, I say. The Colonel laughs and slaps his belly. He says, You wouldn't know what hole to put the key in.

I get my wish. The coyotes turn hind. The Colonel burns rubber. Sailor eats fireflies. My stomach knots. Tongue ties. Head swims. The moon is curved like a fisherman's knife, like a blade that separates the guts from the backbone, the humors from the heart. Morisa and I alone in the moonlight.

THE RUNAWAY NOTE

A THEFT

Morisa and I find Colonel Rip Van Scratch snoring beneath a tree. He's got a long beard like a bib, and an empty can of jet fuel between his legs. There's bowling pins scattered about, and his fingers are three deep in a bowling ball.

Morisa goes through his pockets. He has six versions of my runaway note, a recording of Morisa singing "Auld Lang Syne," and a picture of Sailor Boy. He has a cat in his bag, a bee in his bonnet, ants in his pants, a bird in his hand, and a hole in his heart. He has a shame-cloth, a humble pie, a sin-shifter's collar, a worry stone, and a salvation banner. He has a book on mirrors and another on time travel.

When his pockets are empty, Morisa reaches behind his ear and comes away with the key to the Colonel's van. A butterfly crawls out of his mouth. It flies onto my finger. The butterfly's wings contain words: *It's all done with mirrors. Take a look for yourself. Timely, no?*

THE RUNAWAY NOTE

In the van, we drink the Colonel's jet fuel. We drive aimlessly and shoot his gun at stop signs. We set up his nine-pins and roll the bowling ball. We study his dirty magazines. We park in the cemetery. Morisa sings a song, and I type up a new runaway note.

We roll around in the back of the van. When we're sweaty and satisfied, we look at ourselves in the rearview mirror. Our reflections rock back and forth, back and forth, until we are sleepy. We see the faces of our transmigrations. We see flocks of our selves migrating through time.

It is morning when we awake, each in one of the holes burned by the flying saucers. I cannot explain away my life as a dream, nor my dream as my life. Morisa says, I was dreaming and then I closed my eyes. I say, I opened my eyes and then I was dreaming. I reach for her hand but she has disappeared. And if I pretend that I am only sleeping?

THE RUNAWAY NOTE

THE PAST REFLECTED IN THE KNIFE
MADE OF MIRRORS

I steal the Colonel's van
Morisa rides shotgun
We slice through the night
And the Milky Way
It is a caesarian curtain

Morisa says, Look behind you
I say, Don't ever look back
She stares in the rearview
I say, Do you see the Colonel?
She says, No, I see you and me

I steal a look
And am stabbed by the past
Our bevy of sins and misdeeds
Each one a letter folded and tucked
In the glass envelope of the other

THE RUNAWAY NOTE

I want to jump right in
The back door of our lives
And meet ourselves again, kiss
Morisa for the first time, tongues
Buried beneath the cemetery moon

Our love runs deep
As a knife wound
And when she cuts me loose
It's a sin against time
Like a mother snuffing her own babe

THE RUNAWAY NOTE

THE HOBO & THE GYPSY SAINT

Mother and Daddy make me grow a beard, yet I still feel like a boy. Mother patches my pants, puts white sunglasses over my eyes, and tops it off with a black hat. Daddy sticks a cigar in my mouth and a bindle stick on my shoulder. They pronounce me a hobo and send me door to door to beg for candy.

I soap windows. I throw rotten eggs. I burn tires on Main Street. I set loose Great Grandpop's bumblebees. The hobos and I get chased out of town. We hop a train. The hobos tell me they know of my transgressions. They say, You've broken the hobo code.

I plan to buy off the hobos. I open my bindle stick but they've seen it all before. A picture of a dead boy. The sound of a motorcycle killing a dog. A letter from this or that reincarnation. The head hobo kicks me from the train, saying, Boy, what you lack in imagination you make up in bullshit.

THE RUNAWAY NOTE

I hit the road and meet a band of retired Gypsies. I read their palms. I blacktop their driveway. I plant eggs in a Gypsy baby's nose. She sprouts monarch butterflies, morphs into a woman, and is pronounced a saint.

Saint Morisa. I recognize her instantly. I build Saint Morisa a maze of stairs, and we spend our days ascending and descending. I walk behind and stare at her legs. It's like watching the waves in the ocean.

Saint Morisa says, You look like hobo. I say, I've got a picture of a dead boy, the sound of a motor-cycle killing a dog, and a letter from this or that reincarnation. She is not impressed. I say, I've also got deer antlers, fingernail clippings, and a pinch of unicorn horn.

Morisa's monarchs surround me and fill my mouth and nose. This is just to scare me to do her bidding. She leads us back to the Kaats Kills. Her monarchs battle the bumbles, but it's not much of a fight. The monarchs dodge and dance and the bees make a lot of noise. I say, All this nonsense, it's all for you!

THE RUNAWAY NOTE

She says, If you ever see the face of God, it means that you have died. I say, That's no way to talk about our dream. She says, We knew each other, knew others, but we are not known. With her words the butterflies, bees, and my runaway note swarm in the sky.

I tug on my beard and take a puff from my cigar. She's bored, but she lets me look at her legs. She removes my hat. She removes my bindle. She pretends that we are not on the run. And I pretend that the fiddle that we hear in the distance is not accompanied by drums and howls and a very sad jug, all playing a tune that, in this lifetime, we were never meant to hear.

THE RUNAWAY NOTE

FROM YOUR DROWNING MAN

Morisa, you're buried in our Kaats Kills, yet I feel your phantom hands upon my throat and hear your twangy folk songs. You calm my stutter when I fear I will stammer into the afterlife. From this deserter's prison here in the tropical swamps, I can still see the freckled shape of Libra on your hip, the scales that balanced my words and my heart, the scar in the shape of a star behind your ear. Remember when I first tried to pronounce my love? It came out *la-la-la*, and when you sang those syllables back to me, shivers danced on my skin. I left you only when the Colonel commanded me, and though afraid, I held my post at every battle until I was shot with iron and blasted with fever. I was three months in a hospital—the letter I sent you written in a nurse's hand. Mother wrote back to say that you were in a family way, laid-up in bed, drinking vinegar against the green sickness, something growing inside, even as your skin yellowed. You sang to me—red and red and red— and that's why I ran. I made my escape north, home to the Kaats Kills, to marry you, and to be a father—a true union of three. I ran, feet bare, for a day and slept in a cattle barn. My brothers in arms, found me, poked my chest with gun barrels, laughed as I stuttered my purpose. The Colonel punishes men for family loyalty, and at the prison men choke on promises they didn't keep, drink it down with stinking marsh water. Then another damp letter from Mother: the breech, your funeral, and a winter mountain of grief. Beyond the walls, out where the sea slaps the shore, sharks circle the living and the dead, then leave for the endless sea, and eventual return. When I leave this bodily prison, I will swim through the afterlife, stuttering without you, listening for your twangy lullabies that ease the seizures of tongue and time.

THE RUNAWAY NOTE

THE ALL WET ROMANCE

We drive the Colonel's van to an abandoned house near the dam site. It is white and bowed like a new-pregnant belly. A bark-gray heron stands in the water. I say, Daddy shot one when it ate his pond stock. Morisa says, When you're dead, how do you want your body? I say, I don't want it at all. I tell her about my dead dog and the dug-up kittens. The heron jumps into the wind, a cloud of smoke. I say, Stick my corpse in the crotch of an oak tree. She shows me a scar behind her ear. It looks like a star. I bite my tongue. I pull my rope from my pocket. She says, Sprinkle my ashes on the back of a heron. She says, Climb through the window.

The house is a ghost's head with a smashed-in skull. The window is an empty eye socket. Rot-covered shingles on the porch are broken teeth. We climb inside. We see a stack of books. We see lamps and couches. We see a pile of beaver shit. We see a mouse skeleton. We see a set of teeth. We smell underwater. We feel the dampness of time. The stairs lean like the mast of a sinking ship. A tree branch pokes through the roof like a serpent. Baby socks hang out the dresser like dog tongues. She says, This is my mother's house. She sings to a melted hi-fi and watches a blind-eyed TV. I say, You're a liar. She says, The hair on my belly paves the road to paradise. I say, I know a dead boy. She picks me a rose. She says, Go home.

I drink a pint of gasoline. I smoke the filings from a bored-out piston. I track down Uncle. He works for Conservation as a poacher. He once sexed a bear. He once tamed my aunt. He captures me a heron and charges me twenty dollars. His net breaks its beak. I tie it to a tree at the dam. I take Morisa at nighttime. The moon is a hole in a black door. God is a spy for Mother. When I light a cigarette, my mouth catches fire. The heron hisses like a snake. Morisa says, I'm not even dead yet. I get down on my knees. She has a thimble cup in her belly with black hairs leading down. I take out my knife. The heron spits. It smells like dead salamanders and minnows. I say, I know where the dead live in the reservoir. She says, You're a fiend. I say, I lived here my whole life.

THE RUNAWAY NOTE

At the dam, we take off our clothes. The peepers laugh at me naked. An owl ooos at her thing. It looks like a keyhole in a white door. I see the Devil's eyeball. I ride on the back of a walleye. She straddles a largemouth. We swim a hundred feet deep to Sailor Boy's house. We swim to the drowned girl's house. Gypsies live there. They stole Grandmother's raccoon. It didn't know how to swim. Morisa wants to go back to her mother's. She wants to free the heron. I say, It's dead. The reservoir ghosts sing hymns. We come up from the water. I forget how to breathe. Coyotes run on the top of the dam. Morisa runs with them. They run down the giant staircase. Their laughter runs in S-curves. Water runs downhill. I am from the mountaintop and she is from the valley. The sound of a song is not always where you think it's coming from.

THE RUNAWAY NOTE

DAMPENED SPIRITS

I wake like most mornings to the yipping of coyotes running across the top of the dam. Sailor Boy and I sleep in the spillway, praying for a flood. We're lonely without Morisa. We spend our days throwing sticks and stones, shouting curses, but the dam pays us no mind.

A fossil forest downstream is from the Age of Fish. This was around the time fish started walking and talking and making a fuss. They kept busy making baby fish and donating to the fossil record. They sang love songs. They wrote down their litany of sufferings, shortcomings, and unfulfilled aspirations. They dreamed of swimming and flying.

Sailor Boy and I dream around the fire. I tell Sailor Boy about how when Aunt Saucy babysat, she fed Sister and me franks and beans on plastic dishes. Over crying babies and her programs, Aunt Saucy did not hear my full mouth say, *It's thumbs and pinky tips*. Trapeze artists, we swung on the unanchored swing set. Metal legs pulled from the ground and bit back into dirt. We raced around Aunt Saucy's trailer, finish line a splash of mud above the septic tank. We ran coyote-fast under the moonlight until she called our names. We stripped for baths—lights off—our T-shirts the afterglow of firefly remains. When we giggled past bedtime, Aunt Saucy's boyfriend threatened spankings. I rubbed my hair with a blanket to watch static fireworks. Aunt Saucy and her boyfriend said *Oh God! Jesus!* louder than anyone in church ever did. Crickets and door creaks and Mother and Daddy carried us to the car's cool vinyl seats. Not even a mile drive, I fell back into sleep. Nights at Aunt Saucy's ended as tires pinched familiar gravel, pop and hiss of the turned-off engine. Mother touched her lips to each of my eyelids, and beer-smoke on Daddy's sandpaper face against my face, he carried me up the stairs and put me down to bed, where I dreamed dreams included in my runaway note.

I tell Sailor Boy about Daddy, a Navy man, inked in the Sixties by the famous Sailor Jerry: birds dive on the flowered wall of his chest, topless beauties dance on his calves, island girls bewitch from his biceps, and on his ass are red lips that puckered long before he met Mother. The ink now faded, doctors plot their maps and navigate Daddy's flesh with scalpels and lasers: oxbow of Torn Rotator Cuff, mountain range of Spinal Fusion, volcano of Passed Kidney Stone, and sticky caverns of Blocked Coronary Artery. The birds on Daddy's chest now sing hesitant songs, their feathers wisped gray. They do not trust the backbeat of an aging heart. The once pert nipples of the aloha girls have faded in modesty. Yet they wink, as if to say they are late-night dancers and still have plenty of leg, the kind of girls who laugh in your face when you ask for the last dance.

I tell Sailor Boy about my dreams, about the one where Morisa and I share a last dance near a window and watch the underwater town, its foundations skinned and cut open, splayed in moonlight. Morisa says, Tyro, you're a skinless man, how difficult to keep your company with your more-than-skin-deep beauty. Gut check, she says, more to herself than to me, the skinless man. She says, Your heart beats out of reflex, not desire. She says, This doesn't make me sad as much as it makes me self-conscious. She prefers skin, its shallow depth, its world of illusion, the cover to the book, the wall to the open window. In fact, when dining, she loves the skin more than the meat. Skin, from crispy to burnt—oh! the way it crunches between her teeth and explodes warmth upon her tongue. During a period of glandular over-stimulus, she builds a city from chicken skin and broken hearts. She invites me to dine in the new city's chambers. She starts a conversation about desire. I chew with my mouth open. I wear my heart on my napkin and wipe my hand on my sleeve. I know—all is lost. While I eat dessert, she gathers the feathers of 8000 chickens, and stitches together 1000 veils. When I'm stuffed like a turkey, she presents me with the veils, one at a time. I must wait for each and every one. She says, Just this once, dance like I can't see you.

At night, Morisa returns. Sailor Boy stands on his hands. He tap dances. He does the Watusi. Morisa says, I dreamed I was hanging by my knees from a cliffside tree, and in the dream, I was dreaming of mountain runoff and a sickly mother goat. The mother goat gimps by, braying and bleating, and I wonder if I should help her. Morisa says, I woke and craved mountain goat milk. I drank two-percent cow straight from the carton. Cardboard, pasteurization, homogenization, vitamins A and D. No teat. No goat. No quench. Morisa says, In my dream the travel agents announced specials on cold weather destinations: *PATAGONIA FOR NUDISTS.* I bought a polar bear disguise and broke into the zoo. Scaring off the penguins, I claimed a new home of ice and chilly, chlorinated water. To kill the taste of raw fish, I stuck my tongue to the frozen prison bars. She says, I woke up feeling imprisoned, Tyro. Could it be that I miss you?

I am the happiest runaway in the world. The beating of my heart is like a mad devil banging a gong. My beating heart shakes the earth, rattles windows, rolls cars over. My beating heart breaks the dam. We stand beneath a tidal wave of my affection. This is the flood I have seen in my dreams. Sailor Boy jumps on my back. I reach for Morisa's hand. She says, The world will return to the fishes. And so it does.

THE RUNAWAY NOTE

DEAR PRECIOUS QUEEN OF
OUR HEARTS,

You are loved forever. The tiny bones of your fingers point us to the trees where vultures fan their wings. You say, Trees cannot speak. Vultures are the mouthpiece.

Dear Precious Queen of Our Hearts,

By the light of your wisdom, we dig up the trees and replant them top side down, roots growing toward the sun. Vultures sing their first songs, and the beavers become miners.

Dear Precious Queen of Our Hearts,

We wonder how to regain our rotted bodies, how to snap our fingers or whistle. You say, Clack your bones together, let the wind whistle through your ribs.

THE RUNAWAY NOTE

Dear Precious Queen of Our Hearts,

We hang mason jars on the tree roots to make you a funeral song. We dead are percussionists, tapping a tune on glass timpani, but we will never dance again without you.

THE RUNAWAY NOTE

SPREAD YOUR WINGS

I'd rather not tell you the exact circumstances in which I rendezvous with Colonel Rip Van Scratch, but it does involve a certain plant derivative currently unavailable to the public. The Colonel wants the plant derivative because it induces certain psychosomatic possibilities that the conscious mind prefers remain inactive. Under the Colonel's care, and his scalpel, patients undergo physical transformation typically left to the laggard forces of evolution.

Have you ever seen a woman with a feline face, a waiter with *four* opposable thumbs, a man with a canine's sense of smell? After some conversation about his medical goals, surgery techniques, and clientele, the Colonel invites me to his Intent-Evolution Ranch.

Springtime maples in the Kaats Kills are like Asian jewels. The ranch's buildings rise from the valley floor like hives, and there I reunite with Sailor Boy. We follow a well-worn trail around the ranch grounds.

Sailor Boy says that his cape covers the wings that the Colonel has constructed for him. We stand on a ridge, and Sailor Boy says, I believe I can fly but I am afraid to do so.

Sailor Boy's cape flutters to the ground. The wings match his skin's pigment yet they are covered in stitching scars. Sailor Boy looks as if he might pull apart like perforated paper. He says, I don't trust myself, not with wings anyhow. What if I never want to land?

Later, when I ask the Colonel what frightens Sailor Boy, he shakes his head in disgust. This is why I brought you here, he says. After dinner, the Colonel and I make a serious and substantial transaction. He never mentions the soul I already owe him.

That night, as I sleep in one of the many cottages (the walls a taxidermist's wet dream), I hear a commotion several doors down. Sailor Boy and the

Colonel argue back and forth—the wind pulls their words away from me. I listen in vain. Through the darkness, I see the eyes of a stuffed coyote staring back at me.

I stand on the bed, my arms spread wide as I imagine Sailor Boy might before flight. I consider the music of two wings beating down against the human body, lifting it up.

Mission Control, Sailor Boy says in a voice that seems to come from some height. Mission Control, he says, there will be no touch down. Repeat. Mission Control, there will be no touch down.

The sound echoes the sadness of geese fading north for the summer.

THE RUNAWAY NOTE

MORISA IN THE BATH

Morisa relaxes in the tub while rain pops on the tin roof, and I imagine a lightning strike, a solid plate of blue electricity. Three straight weeks of rain, and when she drains the tub, riverbank rings will remain. Her leg breaks the surface of the water, like Nessie beckoning the paranormal tourists. A wave of a foot and a wiggle of toes is all it takes for me to fetch the camera.

I've seen pictures of Morisa in the bath—bubble baths with her little brother and a rubber duck. I ruin the moment by thinking of grown men with her in the bath or in the shower, or worse, her and a man stark naked at a dam site. She has a thing for dam sites. The tin roof takes the lightning strike, and just like that, we're staring at the dark sky, rain falling in the bathroom. I'd like a foot massage, sir, she says, sinking up to her chin and resting her legs on the tub edge like nothing's happened. She doesn't cover herself or ask me to fix the roof. The teakettle whistles, and since we're evidently not paying attention to the roof, I say, I'll get your tea.

THE RUNAWAY NOTE

My belly aches. An adventurous sort would hop in with her, socks and all, but I steep tea. I cover my head with a towel and wish we lived on a dry planet. We'd be Bedouins, hiding our bodies with great sheets. But no oases, no harems, no genies in bottles. Just a lot of sheep and people making goat cheese. But as a Bedouin, I wouldn't have this: bubbles up to her chin, and when she sits up to reach for the teacup in my hand, bubbles sliding down to reveal breasts, a nipple. I pour the remaining water from the teakettle into the bath; she closes her eyes. She pokes a toe above the water and whispers, Thanks. I hold her wet toe and for some reason my eyes tear up. Look at the roof, I say. I sit down on the toilet to regain my balance. Then I'm up on the roof with a blue tarp and a staple gun, repairing the damage nature thinks is its duty.

Back inside, her skin is soft and pink. She wears only a robe, but I take her hand and lead her outside into the rain. This is so Scandinavian, she says. Immediately her skin is gooseflesh. I take off my shirt and open her robe. We embrace. The water tastes new, our feet sink in the saturated ground. I sidestep, pulling her with me, *almost* dancing. Look down, I say, as water fills our deep and muddy footprints.

Dip me, she says. Without another word, we agree that these imprints will become the fossils through which past and future people will know us.

LITTLE MORISA, NO. 1

One night, Little Morisa told Sailor Boy to fetch my dog. Sailor Boy called the dog's name. He looked in the dog coop. He searched in the fields, in the woods, and in the abandoned house. He swam to the bottom of the reservoir to save the dog if it was drowning. He put an ad in the newspaper. Little Morisa just laughed and laughed 'cause she knew that my dog was already dead, a victim of the Colonel's motorcycle.

LITTLE MORISA, NO. 2

One night, Little Morisa and I reclined in the cemetery. The moon was like God's eye. We sniffed each other like coyotes. The clouds covered the moon. The night turned black. I said, Oh no, I can't see my hand in front of my face. Little Morisa just laughed and laughed 'cause she knew my hand was not in front of my face.

THE RUNAWAY NOTE

LITTLE MORISA, NO. 3

One night, Morisa and I conjured alive a dead boy from a photograph. The townsfolk accused us of being witches. They searched us for third nipples, horns, and other proofs. They threw us in the river to see if we would sink or float. Little Morisa just laughed and laughed 'cause she knew the townsfolk believed in forgiveness, Jesus, and the resurrection of the body.

LITTLE MORISA, NO. 4

One night, Sailor Boy was standing on the street crying. Little Morisa walked over and said, Why the tears? Sailor Boy said, I was dead, but you and Tyro resurrected me. I miss the spirit world. I miss my mother. Little Morisa said, Why your mother's standing right across the street. Sailor Boy jumped up and down and ran to cross the street. The Colonel was speeding by on his motorcycle and hit Sailor Boy, killing him dead. Little Morisa just laughed and laughed 'cause she knew that the woman across the street was not Sailor's mother.

THE RUNAWAY NOTE

LITTLE MORISA, NO. 5

One night, I stole the Colonel's van. The Colonel damned our souls to hell. Little Morisa just laughed and laughed 'cause she knew that we had no souls to damn. I had already traded mine for the red typewriter, and she had traded hers for a singing voice.

LITTLE MORISA, NO. 6

One night, Little Morisa and I stole the Colonel's van. The Colonel sent us a letter saying that if we did not return the Sin Bin in a fortnight our souls would belong to the Devil. Little Morisa just laughed and laughed 'cause she knew that the Colonel was the Devil.

LITTLE MORISA, NO. 7

One night, Little Morisa and I stole the Colonel's van. We were on the run for years, but the Colonel finally caught us and threw us in the slammer. He said that we would be judged in a court of law. Little Morisa just laughed and laughed 'cause she knew that we had broken the law and it couldn't be fixed.

LITTLE MORISA, NO. 8

One night, Little Morisa and I stole the Colonel's van. We were on the run for years, but the Colonel finally caught us and threw us in the slammer. He said that we would be judged by God. Little Morisa just laughed and laughed 'cause she knew that the Colonel was God.

LITTLE MORISA, NO. 9

One night, Little Morisa and I stole the Colonel's van. The Colonel rounded up his men and a pack of bloodhounds to track us down. After years, he captured us. He sentenced us to hanging. Morisa just laughed and laughed 'cause she knew we were already dead.

LITTLE MORISA, NO. 10

One night, Little Morisa and I stole the Colonel's van. We slipped into a shared dream where our souls inhabited bodies we did not remember. The Colonel sent us a letter saying that reincarnation was a sin. Little Morisa just laughed and laughed 'cause she knew that for every sin, you could believe and pray your way to forgiveness.

THE RUNAWAY NOTE

TRESPASSING

Someone has spray-painted *THIS TOWN'S ALL WET* on one side of the dam and *TYRO RULES!* on the other. Morisa says, Sometimes I watch you oscillate between child and man, and I don't know which is mine. I say, I like to live outside the law honestly. She says, Billy the Kid you're not.

We drive to a deserted farm with two signs: *No Trespassing* and *For Sale*. Morisa is hesitant but I insist, so we enter the house. She takes cautious steps and I take souvenirs. A house not living in the present, I say. She hushes me and says, This was someone else's life.

A car slowly passes, and Morisa runs out the back door and through an orchard. She keeps looking back to the road. I say, There's nothing to be scared of. He'll never find us.

She looks at her reflection in the pond. As if in a trance, she says, On this day, a party from Hunter was through Big Hollow peddling shad and herring at forty cents each. Men, boys, and cats ran in all directions with fish. Rip Van Scratch of the Kaats Kills was here trying to sell a new typewriter to our citizens. Lee & Ferris sell ready-made clothing at prices that will make hawkers howl. The fields are pink with milkweed blossom.

I look at my reflection in the pond and feel like I'm falling into a deep sleep. I say, After searching through the woods for stray cattle, Wallace Hall was returning to his home when he discovered a little girl wandering alone. She was taken to her people who had been looking for her since morning. Of late, we have been favored with zero weather.

Morisa, her eyes dreamy, sticks her finger in the pond and says, There are some hoodlums in town who paint discolor cover & conceal their & each of their faces, & do so disguise their & each of their faces so as to prevent themselves from being identified while perpetrating time to the great terror and disturbance of our citizens. If they do not speedily desist, they will be exposed as they are known.

She pulls her finger out of the pond, and it leaves no hole. I say, That's how much they'll miss us. She says, I miss them already. I say, Who? She says, Us?

I say, Keep your eyes from the mirror—Don't look back. Morisa just laughs and laughs. Honestly, her tears are from laughter.

THE RUNAWAY NOTE

SPECTER

Morisa and I leave behind the dying horse, the rifle, and two bread rolls. I see no time for prayer. In a single file, the cavalry travels the road above us. In the distance, smoke rises from our house and barn. On the hill below the road, we run toward the woods. We hear the plod of slow hooves and stop. I tell Morisa to stay low. Hiding in the high grass, we see only the beards and hats of the riders. Keep your head down, I whisper, if you cannot see them, they cannot see you. She is young enough to believe.

Our horse cries its goodbye, and the soldiers rein their living horses, shout, laugh. I lift my head to see riders dismount, and then I take to Morisa's believing, burying my tears in the dirt. Only a few, but their boots in the grass hurt my ears. Morisa's whimper leaves a two-day hunger in my stomach. The Colonel's cigar smells of meanness, and his spit hits the clover—It was I who shot Daddy's rifle from the second-floor window. The Colonel butchers the grass with his sword. He hisses like a vulture. I wet the ground beneath me. When he pulls his sword, the wind gives an achy sigh. Metal sears my thin skin, my sinewy muscle, my growing bones. I am silent but see blue morning glories—a momentary flash—before sharpened steel sinks through my heart.

I was one and now I am two. When you are two, there is no way to know the pain of your other. My living ears never heard Morisa scream, but to my dead ears, it is winter wind stealing through loose windowpanes. I watch as the Colonel kicks my body down the hill—it rolls to the creek bank.

My first day as a dead boy, I stagger and coo my way to the Dubois mansion. The Colonel and his men piled Daddy and the Dubois family in a pit behind the rose garden. Mother and Sailor Boy are forced to serve chicken and bourbon to the killers. The Colonel looks younger without his hat, his fresh shave, but his hair is still like Jesus'. The

THE RUNAWAY NOTE

Colonel dances, and Mother shakes as she pours whiskey. He tosses his cigar on the carpet, and I remember the soldiers setting our cows on fire. Sailor Boy twitches and mutters, and the Colonel laughs until Sailor Boy cries. Murderous bastard, Mother says.

When I squeeze Mother's hand and she doesn't squeeze back, I wonder if the living world is for the dead. She sounds like a scar and looks like a child's scream—there is melting ice at her throat. I smell the iron stains on my back and chest—they are dyes of a different life, that of matter, heft. Daddy leans in the corner, weeping saltless mist. Standing before Daddy, I find that the dead are made of smoke, and their words rub off on your fingers like ash. When Sailor kicks the Colonel, hell breaks loose. Whiskey-breath men grab Mother. Daddy evaporates like fog licked by the morning sun.

THE RUNAWAY NOTE

I stand with my arms open, realizing the living don't know who's going to die, but that some will sooner than others, and it makes them nervous, makes them prone to violence. With my arms open, no ash falling from my mouth, I wish mercy for my family, wish that when they turn to vapor, they will remember me, will touch me, will dance right *in* me like two clouds merging in the sky.

THE RUNAWAY NOTE

SHE RUNS AWAY, NOT IN RETREAT

I wake like most mornings to the cuss and bark of a heron taking flight from the swamp. I hit my head on a hollow log and curse Morisa. The swamp reflects orange and the woods are black and white.

The beaver lodge holds the geometry of my desire and therefore my sadness. I knock on the door. Ole Bucky answers. I say, Where is she? He says, Who? I say, Act like a man, not an owl. He says, I'm a beaver and whomever you're looking for, she's not here. I say, I followed her up Dog Hill, and I saw her go inside. Ole Bucky says, Why didn't you join the party?

I push past him and hear what I do not want to hear: Morisa singing and the beaver band blowing jugs and sawing fiddles. She says, Tyro, come sing with me. I stamp up and down and hit my head on the ceiling. The beavers clap to my beat. I point to Morisa. I point to the door. She looks at me and sticks out her tongue. I poke my head through the roof and walk away, wearing the lodge like a dress.

Morisa says, You look stunning. Very crinoline. She invites me to the prom. A beaver chews on my kneecap. Morisa and I are making up, so she skins his hide and sews a fur suit. In the van, we make awkward love.

At the prom, I kiss the Queen congratulations. Morisa tears apart her beaver-hide suit. She says, You're a cheat. She says, You're a fiend. I sit down to explain, but my dress pops up, revealing hidden beavers who join the party and play their jugs and fiddles. Morisa disappears.

I find her in the van. She says, How could you? I stutter, I stammer. I say, You ran off with a gang of beavers! She says, They're not a gang, they're a family! And besides you know nothing about music or having a good time! I say, That's true, but I love you. She says, I feel trapped. I explain the human condition. She kicks at the sides of the van. I say, Hey, it's paid for! She says, It's stolen! I say, I mean that I pay for my sins as I go.

She runs up Dog Hill, through the woods and to the swamp. I follow in the van and shout her name. I plead for forgiveness. I beg her to stop. The beavers aren't home, I say. She stands at the edge of the swamp. She yips like a coyote. I get down on my knees, my hands held as if in prayer. Not this again, I say.

She says, You'll never learn. I say, You're probably right. She runs on all fours through the woods, which are black and empty like space. Expanding and contracting. When she runs, it is not in retreat but in pursuit. I give chase, meaning that I retreat. I will never catch her. Unless she wants me.

I repeat, I will never catch her.

THE RUNAWAY NOTE

MOCKING

I wake like most mornings at the wheel of the Sin Bin. I drive while dreaming. I drive in reverse and see the past approach behind me. The future, my friends, looks like the moon. I slow down and shift out of contrary. A dog clings to the windshield, and there's a beaver pelt strung to the antenna. Windows down, I hear the coyotes yelping after Morisa's scent. My umbilical cord and a yellow ribbon hang from the rearview mirror.

Morisa buys her perfume at the hunting supply store. She's partial to free samples. She's liable to smell like a fox one day and a doe the next. Scents like that keep the prey praying, the dogs scratching, and the hunters up trees. I bathe in pine needles and the light of the moon. I map the sky with a flashlight. A flying saucer flashes back and asks me to follow. Brighter than the moon, it's shaped like a coyote. I consider my future. I turn on the hazards and take a snooze.

THE RUNAWAY NOTE

I dream of flying saucers and inquisitions. I dream like the crow flies, straight to the point. I dream the Colonel sunk my typewriter at the dam site. I dream I am sinking like an anchor. I dream I am an anchor cut loose. I dream of sin and superstition. I dream of coyotes, heads bowed in prayer. They bark my name, but who listens? My dreams are like a shaving of the tooth that bit me: dirty and in bad taste.

I wake to the past swooping down. It smells like nostalgia and rot. It sounds like a house caving in. I hit the gas and speed into the night. I follow the yelping of the coyotes. I follow the scent of fox. I drive through fog and demonic gloom. The moon wobbles and the stars collide. The sky is the disco to which I was not invited.

A mockingbird lands on my shoulder. It makes the sound of the Colonel's motorcycle. He says, Morisa got a call from her agent and she got the part of a lifetime. I say, Whoopee! I say, Now she'll find some other sucker. I hit the gas, but the Colonel he keeps up. I say, I hope he's rich. I hope he's a Scientologist. The Colonel says, I hear he's good-looking. Oh me! I think. My face it's swollen from an emotion that will heretofore go unnamed. The Colonel says, What now will be your trespass offering?

I awake into a foggy dream to find letters Morisa wrote me long ago. She left a pencil and a book of stamps. History repeats itself, and I am back sending dispatches to her every night. Cigarettes burn and typewriter hums. The coyotes cry for food.

The garden is full of weeds, and the moon is full of whiskey and milk. With the typewriter, I build the world's largest monument to sentimentality and hopelessness. It looks like a stack of paper. It looks like a pile of salt.

THE RUNAWAY NOTE

MORISA'S THIRD FLOOD

Dear Tyro,

Fear not, my voice has haunted these mountains for years, and like a soft wind it now reaches your ears. This undertaking—the delivery of my body in its rotted broadcloth and lace—is nothing new to you. Removal and reinterment. Move me, you must, for soon the third flood will come for me.

You remember the first flood, how the Huntersfield Creek washed away father's funeral parlor and furniture shop. We thought all was lost, but Father sang a different tune, and we, as The Searles Family Singers, performed from New York to Georgia. We returned and settled back in the Kaats Kills, again on the banks of that pitiful stream. I taught at the Prattsville Town School, and you studied and worked with Father, selling furniture to the living and taking inventory of the dead.

THE RUNAWAY NOTE

You, Dear, have always been my favorite, and I call not to exhume your memory. That Sunday—the first day of June—before the flood took me, I played the organ and you sang. The Methodist Church had never heard a more heavenly rendition of "Have Thine Own Way, Lord." Do you remember the joke we shared before retiring that evening? Martin's Tailor Shop at the east end of town had the sign that read *Satan Died Here*. You kidded me about how the Martins had been my students—and the Martins fifty years my age! I wanted to tell Mrs. Martin that the sign should say *Satin Dyed Here*. But we heard the cloudburst, and in minutes the deluge ripped the house from the foundation, and it floated downstream, sad and broken. I know you saw the timber, Tyro, saw it strike me down, and if I could ask the Lord to change one thing, it would be that. I know how that image haunts you.

Know that I died instantly. My body, Dearest, was an earthly vessel, but I stayed with it for the twenty-five-mile journey, until I ran aground with the driftwood in Fultonham. From my dead, drenched body, I saw you rescued near the Penn's store. You screamed my name, and I wish I could have blown you a kiss goodbye. I floated with the Disbrow house, the Howard's, and eventually the Van Dusen's; they, too, lost everything. The water carried me through Prattsville, past Gilboa—my birthplace and future grave—Blenheim, and as I reached Fultonham, I lay face up, and I swear God's tears struck my face. I grant Him his sorrow, but my forgiveness He has yet to earn.

I sin, Tyro, even in death. Poor Mother and Father, I was the second of their children to die. Pete was the first, sacrificed in the Southern Rebellion. Forty-seven years I've heard you sing "Have Thine Own Way, Lord," and yet I miss you. I ask Him, Why was I sacrificed? The Lord answers with another flood, one made by men.

Now before the water comes for me again, you've come to replant me, like Mother replanted her peonies after the first flood. I know of the dam they plan to build, how this small town will be under water. This the town where my parents were married and buried. You're replanting them too.

The town will become reservoir, water for the living, for New York City, so far away. You are still a beauty, the wrinkles upon your skin, nothing but ripples on your calm face. Sixty-two years, my love, and I in the ground for forty-seven.

Dear Tyro, from this ground, where we were born, and where I am now buried, exhume me, and lay me to rest on high. Tyro, is it foolish to say that I fear water and rain, that I fear the Lord's Own Way?

THE RUNAWAY NOTE

THE CONFESSION

I stole Colonel Rip Van Scratch's van
the one he calls the Sin Bin
the one he drives real slow down Main Street
eyeing the girls and old ladies.

I stole Colonel Rip Van Scratch's van
the one he calls the Sin Bin.
I stole the Devil's van
and Morisa rode shotgun.

I stole the Colonel's van
'cause the door was unlocked.
I stole the Colonel's van
'cause the keys were in it.

I stole the Colonel's van
'cause the moon was full.
I stole the Colonel's van
'cause my heart burned.

THE RUNAWAY NOTE

I stole the Colonel's van
'cause Morisa told me to.
I stole the Colonel's van
'cause of the mattress in back.

I stole the Colonel's van
'cause I've got a screw loose.
I stole the Colonel's van
'cause of exposure to radon.

I stole the Colonel's van
'cause of photos of Morisa and me
naked in the cemetery
with ghosts watching.

I stole the Colonel's van
'cause a dead boy crawled
from between Morisa's legs
and coyotes gave chase.

THE RUNAWAY NOTE

I stole the Colonel's van
to find the dead boy.
I stole the Colonel's van
'cause in the rearview
I could relive the past
and kiss Morisa
for the first time again.

I stole the Colonel's van
out of malice
out of selfishness
out of my belief in youth.
I stole the Colonel's van
'cause my wires are crossed.
I stole the Colonel's van
'cause there's a law against it.

When you come for us
we'll be waiting.
You expect a big chase scene
a shoot out with plenty of red.
But this isn't the movies, fool.

THE RUNAWAY NOTE

When we see the whites of your eyes
we'll step through the mirror
knife into the past
cut into the marrow of a story
poem.
They'll say we're nostalgic.
But we never cared much
what the neighbors think.

THE RUNAWAY NOTE

GOOD SAMARITAN

I am at the wheel when the van breaks down. Colonel Rip Van Scratch pulls up on his motorcycle. He asks, What's the trouble? I say, It sprung a leak! The wheel fell off! I blew a casket!

He says, I'll go get the jumper cables. I say, There's nothing wrong with the battery. He claims I'm prone to deception, so I ask him to see it my way. He turns a blind eye. He turns in a circle. He turns in a winning ticket. He turns into a Civil War officer and asks for my license and registration.

I say, I bought this here van from a pack of coyotes. I say, Hey, have you seen a girl about this high? Real pretty in the face and legs? She ran off with coyotes. I haven't seen her since.

THE RUNAWAY NOTE

This high? the Colonel says. He pulls out a wanted poster and there's Morisa's face. He says, Stay away from her, for her soul is the coolant that prevents my valves from sticking. He laughs and says, I've had her three ways on a Sunday!

Now I'm mad. I say, Knock, knock. He says, Who's there? I say, Morisa. He says, Morisa who? I say Mortician's what you're going to need if you keep flapping that fool tongue.

I start the van and drive away. I don't look behind me. Every road is long enough to lead you back to your sorrow.

THE RUNAWAY NOTE

TO RENT & TAX THE BODY

God cuts the road for every man's path, or so you said, Tyro, nearly every day of your cowardly life. Even now in the hereafter, you count every stone you ever laid to the walls of your 160 acres. You remember the morning the tin horns blew loud throughout the mountains. Sheriffs Moore and Wright showed up at ten in the morning to collect the rent, thirty-two dollars. Figuring I earned the money churning butter, I grabbed the bills you meant to hand over and stuck them down my bodice, where you had once wandered, believing the boarder's goods belonged to you. After my loss, you no longer cut that road. By noon the Calico Indians arrived, masked and drunk and stinking, their guns drawn, ready to take vengeance. I knew them each to a man. My fingers stitched many of their calico dresses, and I had cut the tails of Starlight and Fancy—the piebald horses you abused—and braided the hair for the masks. You and your dried wife watched me and never lifted a finger. By the time the tenant-baiter Colonel Rip Van Scratch and Constable Edgerton rode their bays up the hill, I donned the calico and a mask myself. I

90

took your gun from the house, Tyro, and extracted the souls of two soulless men—I saw nothing more than a small fog rise from their bodies. Dead, Tyro. You and the others spent years in Sing Sing, and you came back holier than you had ever been. We aren't different these days, Tyro, you counting each and every stone in the walls, and me digging for the dead baby I birthed from your seed, the babe you planted somewhere on this 160 acres. Did we learn, Tyro, what it means to own, to rent, to tax the body and the ones we love? They can't extract money from us when we're dead, can they? But that don't make loss any less. All I ask for is one little thing to hold and call my own. I swear, I'd free her as soon as I touched her bird-size bones.

THE RUNAWAY NOTE

HUE AND CRY

I am on the run again for it is true that I did not float, nor did I sink. I swam downriver. I was trout swift and then took to land faster than a fisher cat. But now I hear the Colonel and his men, their pockets jangling with shotgun shells, their bloodhounds giving tongue, my scent their quest, my blood their reward.

I search for a hiding place in a dark and empty barn. Two eyes flash gold like a wildcat's. I say, Are those the eyes of my killer? The eyes blink in code, and Morisa steps into the light. They tried to drown me, she says. I say, To see how much they will miss us, stick your finger in the pond, and when you pull it out look at the hole.

Morisa licks my face. No one has ever been so happy to see me. I begin to say something romantic, like We're like Trojan moons, you and I. But Morisa taps my shoulder and says, You're IT! She disappears down a hay chute. I shout, This is no time for hide-and-seek! But she has and I shall.

THE RUNAWAY NOTE

I give chase. I've dreamed this dream before. I've played hide-and-seek here time without end. Outside, the Colonel calls my name and spits tobacco juice. I sniff out Morisa's perfume. It tastes like sarsaparilla spiked with snakeroot. The Colonel does not know of her presence, and as I run out of the barn, I pray Morisa will always remember my forfeit.

My drunk assassins let loose like furloughed monks at an orgy. A slug passes through my hand. I put my palm to my face, and my killers are framed in a circle of meat. And how, I silently ask, will Morisa read my palm? I run, the wind whistling Dixie through my hand-hole and bullets singing death.

I steal a bicycle, and those bastards keep shooting. Morisa! Morisa! I want to cry, but she is on her own now, her fate a mystery to me. I was their prisoner once before, and I shall not be again. But how to explain when they are closing in? If I had my typewriter, I would stab out a letter to you.

THE RUNAWAY NOTE

Dear So and So:

We had wonderful times, you and I. Oh, to hold hands while one of us dies, to feel the life force departing. Do remember that you can never both a hider and a seeker be. In such endeavors, please choose carefully.

THE RUNAWAY NOTE

FLASH

Dear Morisa,

Fifty years ago, you predicted my death, and now I've come for you, one last message scrawled across your aging flesh. Go to the looking glass and begin to read the pictures that, with a needle powered by a bichromate battery, I painted on your skin in India ink. Your mother's name upon a cross, she that died in the flood, where your child, too, was pulled from your arms and drowned. Cradle rocking in the treetop. You survived, hauled to land by your long, blonde hair, locks that you've since cut and stowed beneath your bed like a length of rope that might again save you. The spider webs upon your shoulders, the snare of our love, of our grace unto God, His nets casting us together. Two monarchs butterflies on your arms, our migration across America. The frog upon your belly a symbol of our metamorphosis, the snake encircling it, our yield to temptation. Your back is the site of the Last Supper, with the words, *Do unto others as you would*

THE RUNAWAY NOTE

that they should do unto you. And that is why I have come, dear Morisa. As you did for me, I now do for you. The last tattoo I gave you, a vulture with an envelope in its beak. You now see that you've been holding the letter in your hand. You read my words that I wrote so long ago. Come to me now, darling, take my hand, and may we forever Rest in Peace.

—Yours forever, Tyro

THE RUNAWAY NOTE

THE CHARGES

The Jurors of the People on their oath do present that Morisa & Tyro together with diverse other evil disposed persons to the number of ten & to the jurors aforesaid unknown with force & arms unlawfully wickedly willfully feloniously riotously & tumultuously did assemble & gather together to disturb the peace of the People and did then & there paint discolor cover & conceal their & each of their faces, and did so disguise their & each of their faces & persons as to prevent themselves from being identified and did then & there arm themselves with swords dirks guns rifles pistols & other offensive weapons, and while so having their & each of their faces painted discolored covered & concealed, and their & each of their persons so disguised as aforesaid, and being so then & there unlawfully riotously & feloniously assembled & gathered together as aforesaid and being armed with swords dirks guns rifles pistols & other offensive weapons did then & there make great noise riot tumult & disturbance for a long space of time to wit ensuing

97

to the great terror & disturbance not only of the good people then & there inhabiting residing & being but of all other good people then & there passing & repassing along the public streets & highways in contempt of the said people & their laws & contrary to the provisions of the act entitled "an act to prevent persons appearing disguised & armed" against the form of the statute & of said act in such case made & provided and against the peace of the People & their dignity.

THE RUNAWAY NOTE

THE LAND OF THE DISAPPEARED

We are on the run again. Morisa, Sailor Boy, and me. Sailor Boy sees the depot sign and says, This is Nevermore. Morisa says, That's not a name, it's a feeling. I say, We are called the Disappeared. We enter a tunnel and all I see is the flash of Morisa's mouth like a meteor shower gaining on my lips.

In the Land of the Disappeared there's no pretending. We're as good as gone, but we don't worry about God. He's a bit like a cousin running through the woods at night: nobody quite knows where He goes, what He does, or how He manages to keep account of the cows. He hasn't bothered to say as much as one word to us in years.

In the tunnel, Morisa's tongue tastes like moss on a boulder in a shaded wood. That is to say sweet and cool, and if it weren't for the light at the end of the tunnel, we might make good on all we promised.

THE RUNAWAY NOTE

I say, We don't return from the Land of the Disappeared. When the van hits the end of the road that's it. We won't see each other again. Not you and me. Not you and Sailor Boy. Not Sailor and me. Do the math, I say. No pretending.

Sailor Boy says, Nevermore, and then again, like Never More, and I make the mistake of reading something into it, like wondering why we would ever want anything else. The valley below is like a truth you get to the bottom of.

THE RUNAWAY NOTE

THE END OF THE ROAD

Colonel Rip Van Scratch's van is called the Sin Bin, and I am at the wheel. Morisa rides shotgun. The headless Colonel gives chase on horseback. He says, Goddamn are you not tired of the chase?

Indeed, we are weary. Scratch's dirty books are filled with so many incantations to recite and the rearview offers so many incarnations and transmigrations to explore. Morisa's lips are chapped from speaking spells and sucking face. I reach to take her hand and she spits out butterflies. She holds the photograph from which we brought Sailor Boy back to life. He is shivering in the back, and like us, wants to be still. Morisa says, The magic, it only works one way. You can *run away*, but you can never *run return*.

A canyon opens up before us. I look in the mirror and there is the Colonel. The past is brewing up, Morisa and I in all our transmigrations, all our trickery. Our past a recipe for disaster. I know some people live with it, but I've never had the guts. The past is a parasite living off the present. It is the ballast that the pirates of time tie to your feet before they throw you over. Anchors aweigh!

I hit the gas and say to Morisa, I, Tyro of the red typewriter, do pledge myself to your wanton ways, to every cell of your body dead, living, and dying! Morisa just laughs and laughs. Sailor Boy cries, Hurrah! We each spew streams of butterflies.

The van hits the lip of the canyon. I had imagined sailing up, like they do in the movies, but it's nothing like that. The van noses down, and we speed towards the bottom, a sustained and distorted note from a fiddle. In the rearview, I see the full moon getting smaller. The man in the moon recites my runaway note, and I howl my apologies.

Born and raised in the Catskill Mountains, Tyrone Jaeger lives on Beaverfork Lake, Arkansas, with his wife and daughter. His writing has appeared in the *Oxford American, Toad Suck Review, Exquisite Corpse Annual, Southern Humanities Review, West Branch Wired, The Literary Review,* and elsewhere. He is the recipient of the Frank O'Connor Award for Short Fiction, the Theodore Christian Hoepfner Award, and the 2018 Porter Fund Literary Prize. As an undergraduate, he attended Rollins College, and he received his PhD from the University of Nebraska-Lincoln. He has been a member of the faculty at Hendrix College since 2008. He is the author of the short story collection *So Many True Believers.* Visit his website: tyronejaeger.com.